For my Dada

&

anyone who needs a little help with letters and spelling

Published By Priya Desai

Priya Desai
Box 226
30 Red Lion Street
Richmond upon Thames
Surrey
TW9 1RB
www.priyadesai.co.uk

ISBN   978-0-9565247-1-3

Typeset in Plantin Infant

Designed by Flit, London
www.flitlondon.co.uk

Illustrations by Emma Hockley
www.emmahockleyarts.co.uk

British Library Cataloguing in Publication Data
A catalogue record of this book is available from the British Library

Printed in the UK by Empress Litho, London
www.empresslitho.com

Jake Monkey-Tail

by Priya Desai

Illustrations by Emma Hockley

HAVE YOU EVER struggled to spell a word?

Have you ever heard a word and thought,
'Oh that's easy to spell', and then you
sound it out really carefully, spell it, and
an adult can't read it?

Have you ever made a card for someone,
then they can't read the message inside?

They can't even read 'love' or your 'name'!

Well, I'm glad I'm not alone then!

Let me introduce myself. My name is Jake and
I live in a fabulous place called Monkey Jungle.

Lots of monkeys live in Monkey Jungle. You can tell
just by the name! We do have other jungle animal
neighbours as well though, like elephants, giraffes
and panthers. So, Monkey Jungle is really a very
multi-animal sort of place.

Art

I'm only a little monkey, so that means that I have to go to Monkey School every day, except for Saturday and Sunday. I actually like school because I have lots of monkey friends there that I love to play with. I like learning most things like Art, History and Maths, which is my **absolute favourite!** Don't you just **love** numbers?

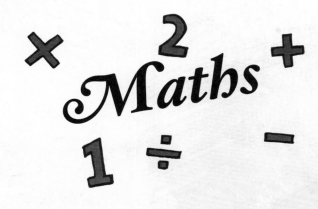

There is just one thing that I find difficult. Spelling...yes...spelling.

Shhh! It's a secret! But at least I can write my letters beautifully. Look I'll show you, here is the alphabet:

o, d, c, b, ə, t

"See, it's perfect...I think."

Every Friday I have a spelling test. Do you have a test on Friday as well? One week I do okay, you know, get 2/10 and the next week I might get 1/10, and on a really bad week I might get 0/10.

I've got another secret to tell you...

Shhh! I'm feeling really worried and scared. It's Friday and I have a spelling test and I told you, "I CAN'T SPELL!"

I try very hard to learn my spellings every week but my teacher can never read them!

I've decided to walk to school really slowly instead of swinging, which is the quickest way of course, because I want to miss the test.

Jake suddenly heard a bell ringing.
It was 9AM and time for school.
Jake quickly swung to school
and sneakily, swung through
the classroom window before his
teacher could notice.

"Good morning, little monkeys," said Miss Emma Monkey, Jake's teacher.

"Today is Friday. I hope you have all learnt your spellings! We will be starting the test in five minutes. Get your pencils ready!"

All the little monkeys silently sharpened their pencils while Miss Emma Monkey handed them a piece of paper, with the numbers one to ten written in the left margin.

"Let's begin," said Miss Emma Monkey. "Number one is...*bat*."

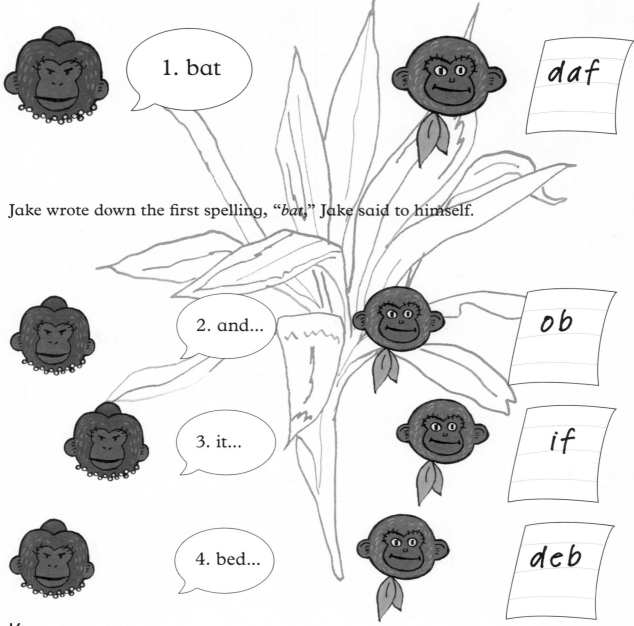

1. bat

daf

Jake wrote down the first spelling, "*bat*," Jake said to himself.

2. and...

ob

3. it...

if

4. bed...

deb

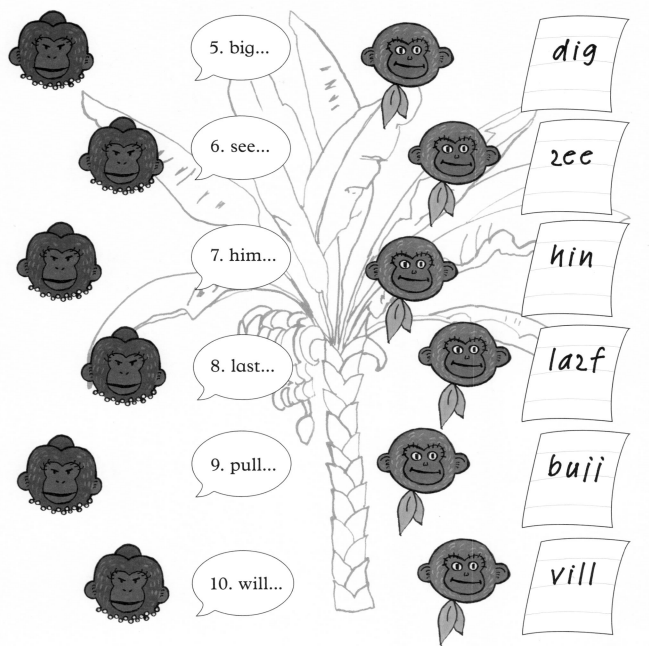

At the end of the day, Miss Emma Monkey
called Jake to her desk.

"Jake you got 0/10 for your spelling test today.
Did you even look at your spellings and
practise? Or were you out swinging around
Monkey Jungle?" asked Miss Emma Monkey.

"But I did look at my spellings and for
a very long time!" said Jake.

"Well, you need to try harder. Take
your test home and show your mother
and father. Off you go!"
said Miss Emma Monkey.

After school that day, Jake walked home slowly. He knew
his mum would ask about his test straightaway, "How did
the test go Jake?" she would say, "Today you did it, didn't
you? 10/10 finally!" and with a big monkey smile Jake
would say, "GREAT mum!"

"I'm not going to cry...I'm not going to cry," said Jake,
holding back his tears. I'm not going to cry..." Jake took
some deep breaths. "There, the tears have gone. I'm OK!

I'm a brave, strong, tough, sporty monkey. I'm going to be the best speller in the whole of Monkey Jungle," said Jake as he began to swing through the trees.

BRAVE

STRONG

TOUGH

SPORTY

Jake loved swinging, it helped clear his mind. Right now, he had many different feelings in his head and heart. And all at the same time! Jake's heart was feeling sad because he wanted to be a perfect speller. And his head was feeling frustrated that he could not spell.

Jake wasn't really thinking about where he was going. He wanted to swing for a little while before he went home to tell his mum about the test. Before Jake knew it, the sun was setting. It was time to go home!

He looked around him but none of the trees looked familiar.

"Oh no! Where am I?" thought Jake. "Which way did I go?" Jake was puzzled.

"Mmm...I have no idea. Well I see the sunset every night on my way home. I'll just go that way."

Jake had been swinging for about five minutes.

He stopped and looked around. He did not know these trees! He didn't recognise them! He looked around again, and this time he saw lots of bright lights in the distance.

"Monkey Town," said Jake as he set off again.

Jake had almost reached the bright lights.

Although he quickly realised that wherever he was swinging to, was not Monkey Town.

These bright lights were far too dazzling to be Monkey Town lights! But Jake could not stop himself; these lights were just **too** fascinating. He just had to see for himself, and with one last swing he had arrived in...in...Jake couldn't describe what was in front of him, letters, dazzling letters, a dazzling Letter Jungle in Monkey Jungle!

All around him were hundreds of letters, all different sizes, hanging from vines. He wasn't sure what they were made of, either the shiniest glass ever or precious sparkly diamonds.

Jake jumped down to the ground so he could have a closer look. He looked up and said to himself, "Let me find a **J** for Jake, that's me!"

He found a sparkly **J** and gently pulled it towards him. He felt proud holding the first letter of his name. **J**ake traced his finger over the shape of the **J**. His **J** for Jake, felt as smooth as a banana and cocoa smoothie!

Jake immediately thought, "If only I could take this amazing **J** home!"

He pulled the **J** and nothing happened. He pulled again...nothing happened.

Suddenly, out of nowhere, appeared an elderly looking monkey, in fact he looked like a grandfather monkey!

"Young monkey...mmm. Young monkey, what are you doing?" said the old monkey.

"I was just admiring your...these...are they yours? Well, I was just admiring your sparkly letters?" said Jake.

"Well, young monkey, you can't take them! These letters are precious, just look at them, look how they sparkle and dazzle...do you know where you are?" said the old monkey.

"Somewhere in Monkey Jungle?" said Jake.

"Yes, this is a very sacred place and it's a SECRET. Shhh! You are in Spellalibrary Junction. There is a library of thousands of letters here, so monkeys can learn to spell. The only monkeys allowed here, are Headmaster monkeys, Headmistress monkeys and monkey teachers. They come here, to find out how to teach young monkeys to learn letters, write letters and then spell. The wisest monkey teacher in the whole of Monkey Jungle's history, created Spellalibrary Junction, and he was called, 'Spelladictionary Monkey' because he could spell any word."

"Oh WOW!" said Jake "Oh WOW, I'm in a secret place. Wait till I tell all of my monkey friends!"

"Oh no you must not, please, you must keep this place a secret, young monkey. If all the monkeys in Monkey Jungle find out about Spellalibrary Junction, they will all come here to learn to spell. They will swing around and then all the diamond letters will be ruined!"

"Oh," said Jake. "Can I tell you a secret, Mr Monkey?"

"Yes of course," said the old monkey.

"Well...well...I....I can't spell," said Jake quietly.

"Sorry, I didn't hear what you just said," said the old monkey.

"I CAN'T SPELL!" shouted Jake.

"There, I've told you my secret. Ooh, that felt quite nice. I CAN'T SPELL! I can't spell!" said Jake with confidence.

"Will you help me, teach me the secret to spelling?" "Please?" asked Jake, with a charming monkey smile.

"I always do so badly in my spelling tests. I never get more than 2/10. Today I got 0/10 and next week, who knows?" said Jake.

Jake looked at the old monkey with a pleading face.

"Mmm...Okay, but you have to keep this all a secret. I'm Spelladictionary Monkey VII. Nice to meet you," said the old monkey as he extended his hand out to Jake.

"Jake, I'm Jake Monkey," said Jake.

"Well, Jake Monkey, come back tomorrow. I must be going. I have work to do, lots of letters to polish," said Spelladictionary Monkey VII as he started to shuffle away.

"But wait, how will I find this place again?" asked Jake.

"You will find a way," shouted Spelladictionary Monkey VII.

The next day, Jake got up extra early. He was a good monkey and he quickly ate his banana cereal to give him energy to swing really fast. He thought starting his journey from school would be the best way to retrace his swings from yesterday.

When Jake arrived at school, he looked for the distant patch of dazzling lights. He could see nothing.

Jake had an idea! His tail was always good at helping him out and getting a sense of things. He held it up and swung it around, left, right, where did his tail want to go? Left felt normal, right felt all tingly.

"Right, I'm going right," said Jake as he started swinging.

When Jake arrived at Spellalibrary Junction, Spelladictionary Monkey was waiting for him. "Perfect timing," he said. "Well, let's get started, we will start with the basics. Can you recite the alphabet?" asked Spelladictionary Monkey.

"Easy, a, b, c, d, e, f, g, h..." continued Jake confidently.

"Perfect, now let's try spelling," said Spelladictionary. "I know this may sound strange Jake, but please spell an **a** in the mud."

Jake squatted on the ground and traced an **a** in the mud.

"Ok," said Spelladictionary Monkey looking puzzled. "Try **J** for Jake."

"Ooh, that's easy. It's a line, and I think a roof," said Jake as he traced.

"Yes, kind of!" said Spelladictionary Monkey. "What have you spelt so far?"

"**aj**", said Jake proudly.

"Well, at least you can read Jake!" said Spelladictionary
Monkey positively.

"Jake, I'm going to teach you how to spell in a new way.
We are not going to use pencils to start with. I will teach
you a different way to spell, because I think using a
pencil and paper, like you do at school, is not helping you
learn your letters very well. We will find a NEW way to
learn letters and to spell. We will find the best way for
YOU Jake!"

"Jake, for every letter of the alphabet, we are going to
write in the mud, make the letter with your tail and then
use a sparkly, diamond letter! Are you ready?"
asked Spelladictionary Monkey.

"Jake, let's start with **a**. Now copy me," said Spelladictionary Monkey.

They traced an **a** together.

Jake was good at copying.

"Good **a** Jake, now let's use our tails. First, hold your tail and make a circle shape with it. Next, place the end of your tail at the bottom of the circle on the right side, which is the side furthest away from you."

Jake copied Spelladictionary Monkey.

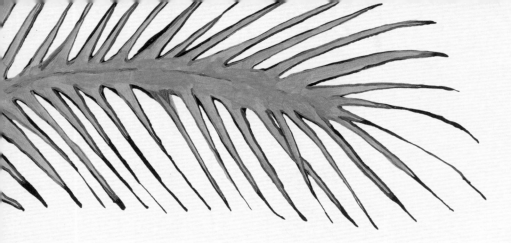

"That's great Jake! You are ready for the fun part. Look up and find me a diamond **a**," said Spelladictionary Monkey.

Jake looked up, there were so many dazzling letters, "I've found one, here it is, it looks just like my **a**," marvelled Jake.

"Well done Jake! Now, do you see where the diamond **a** shines the most?" asked Spelladictionary Monkey.

"Yes, on the corners," said Jake.

"That's right Jake, on the corners and on the bottom right side. That is your outline for **a**, it's like a pattern you can follow."

"Let me mark on the mud where the diamonds shine the most."

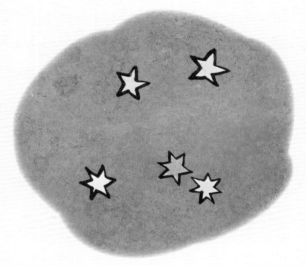

"If you join the dots you will have an **a**. There you go,"
said Spelladicitonary Monkey.

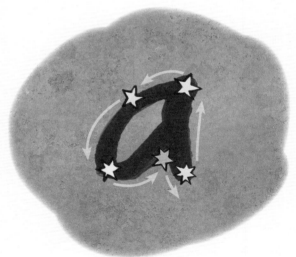

"Now, look at the sparkly diamond **a** again," said Spelladictionary Monkey.

"I want you to remember, where the shiny diamond clusters are for the **a**, and also the shape they make. When you are ready, close your eyes, and look for them in your mind...do you see a picture of the diamond clusters for **a**...? Are the diamond clusters sparkly...? Do you see the shape for **a**...?" asked Spelladictionary Monkey.

"Wait," said Jake as he stood with his eyes tightly squeezed together.

"Yes...yes I do, four dots...four diamond clusters, shaped like a square, and then a cluster on the right side at the bottom. Look, I'll show you!" said Jake, with his eyes still tightly shut, as he made the letter with his tail.

Then Jake automatically wrote an **a** in the air with an imaginary pencil.

"Jake, open your eyes," said Spelladictionary Monkey.

Jake opened his eyes. Had he been dreaming?

"Jake, you have just learnt to spell **a** in a magical way. You have used the mud to write an **a** and feel how the **a** is made...you used your tail, so you can feel the **a** being made with your body, and follow its shape. I've added that bit for fun Jake! It does work, I promise you! And you have used a special part of your brain, that sort of acts like a camera and takes pictures, so you can remember the shape for an **a**. The beautiful, sparkly, diamond clusters have helped you make this picture."

"WOW, I can write an **a**. That was fun! I want to learn **b** now," said Jake enthusiastically. "I'm going to learn to spell!" said Jake as he danced around.

"Wait a second, I want to see if you can remember **a**," said Spelladictionary Monkey.

"Oh, that's easy, **a**, like **a** for apple. I'll show you. I see four diamond clusters," said Jake as he started to shape his tail.

"Then a diamond cluster on the side, at the bottom. This part is away from me," said Jake as he made the little tail of his **a**. "Ooh, this feels funny," chuckled Jake. "And here's an **a** in the mud."

"Brilliant Jake, you are ready for **b**," said Spelladictionary Monkey.

So, in this way, Jake and Spelladictionary Monkey worked through the alphabet every Saturday morning. Jake was a quick learner. He found this new way of learning letters and then spelling, a lot easier than learning in a class with lots of other young monkeys and only using a pencil and paper! Jake also found it easier, to figure out which sound went with each different letter shape. Jake did not know this before. He now knew that this was why, he kept on getting most of his spellings wrong!

Of course, Spelladictionary Monkey did give Jake homework. The first, was to spell the alphabet every day with his tail. The second, was to practise his weekly spelling test using the mud, his tail and also his special 'mind writing', where he has to picture the diamond clusters for each letter. Jake loved to use his tail to practise spelling more than any other way.

Spelladictionary Monkey's lessons were really helpful and week by week Jake's spelling test scores got better and better.

A few months later, after a tough Saturday spelling test, Spelladictionary Monkey said, "Jake, I think you are ready. You don't need me anymore. You can spell! You just passed my spelling test with flying colours! And you could even spell 'impossible'."

"But I love coming to see you Spelladictionary Monkey! My lessons are really helping me with my spellings and what if I forget...?" asked Jake, with a worried look on his face.

"You won't forget Jake, because you have a clever monkey brain! Your brain has taken pictures of all the diamond clusters for each letter of the alphabet. And your tail knows all the letters, or rather *you know* how to make your tail shape the letters. You will never forget now. I promise you. Just keep practising! You are a bright young monkey, I am very proud of you!" said Spelladictionary Monkey as he gave Jake a big monkey hug.

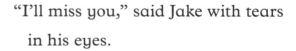

"I'll miss you," said Jake with tears in his eyes.

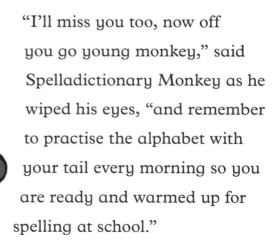

"I'll miss you too, now off you go young monkey," said Spelladictionary Monkey as he wiped his eyes, "and remember to practise the alphabet with your tail every morning so you are ready and warmed up for spelling at school."

The next Friday, Jake swung to school as fast as he could. He was excited about the test; he knew that today was going to be the day he would get 10/10. Jake could feel a tingle in his tail.

"Today is *my* day," said Jake as he sat down for the spelling test.

Jake was focused and feeling confident. His listening ears were ready as he heard Miss Emma Monkey say the first word…"dog".

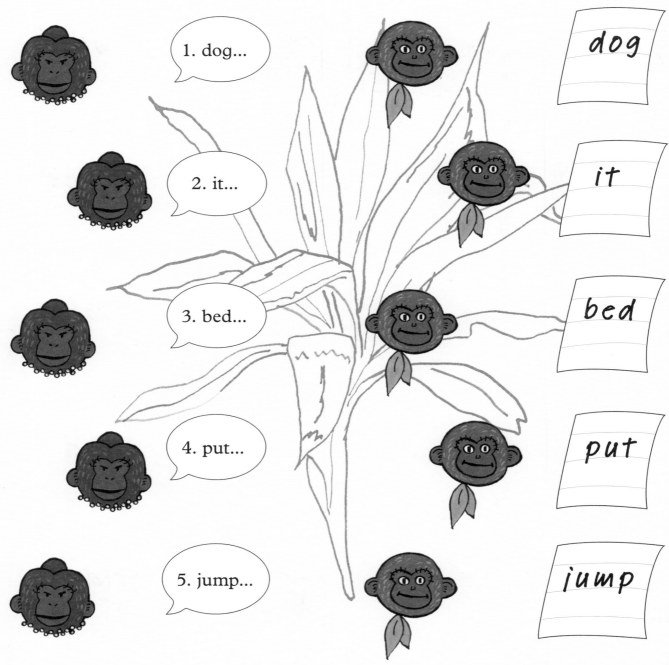

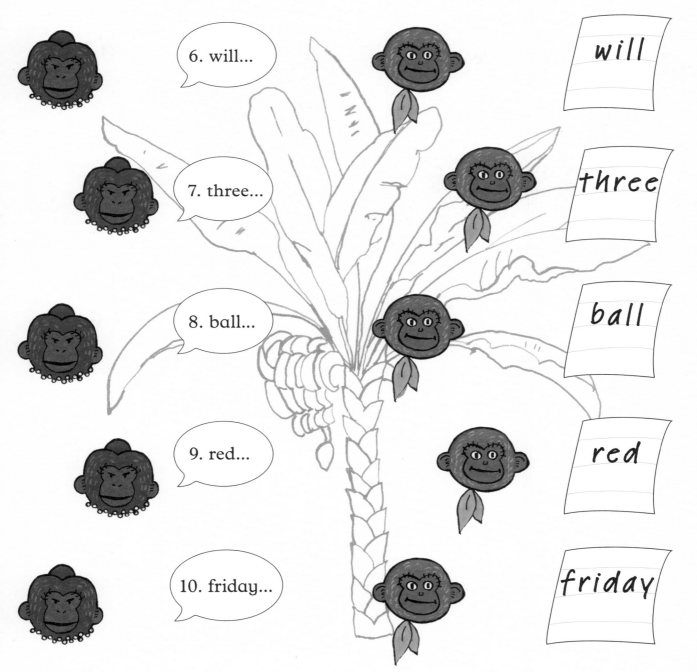

The test was over so quickly and Jake was feeling very pleased with himself.

"Class, leave your tests on the table. It's time to go outside and have a play," said Miss Emma Monkey.

Miss Emma Monkey picked up Jake's test and had a quick look. She was not expecting anything impressive from Jake, but today she had to look again. She needed to sit down! Miss Emma Monkey went through each spelling... **perfect...perfect...perfect!** She was AMAZED. Jake had got his first **10/10!**

Miss Emma Monkey ran outside and shouted for Jake, "Jake Monkey, Jake Monkey, come here right now!" Jake heard his name and with a few swings, he was by Miss Emma Monkey's feet. "Jake you got 10/10 for your spelling test today! Well done!!"

Jake smiled his biggest smile and said, "Yes, I did it! 10/10, 10/10! I have got my first 10/10! **I can spell! I can spell! I can spell!** Please can I see the test, Miss Emma Monkey?"

Miss Emma Monkey showed Jake his test. Jake felt so proud and he couldn't wait to go home and tell his mum and dad.

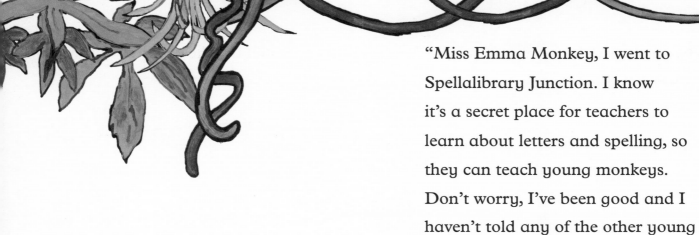

"Miss Emma Monkey, I went to Spellalibrary Junction. I know it's a secret place for teachers to learn about letters and spelling, so they can teach young monkeys. Don't worry, I've been good and I haven't told any of the other young monkeys," said Jake.

"Jake, don't be silly, Spella...Spella... this Spella place does not exist. We learn about teaching young monkeys at Monkey Jungle School for Teachers. Really Jake, you do make up such ridiculous stories! You are just over excited because you got 10/10. Make sure you come and collect your golden monkey sticker at the end of the day. Your *first ever* golden monkey sticker!" said Miss Emma Monkey as she affectionately patted Jake on the head.

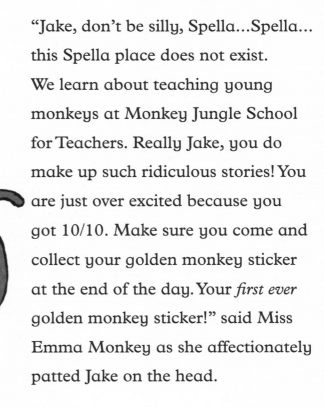

At the end of the day, Jake went to Miss Emma Monkey's desk and politely asked for his golden monkey sticker. He looked at the sticker carefully, the monkey looked so familiar…"Spelladictionary Monkey VII!!!" Jake whispered to himself.

"Miss Emma Monkey, Miss Emma Monkey, who is this monkey?" asked Jake excitedly.

"It's Spelladictionary Monkey, he set up Monkey Jungle School for Teachers," said Miss Emma Monkey.

"But…I know him…I know him!" said Jake.

"Don't be silly Jake; he lived hundreds of years ago. You are just over excited," said Miss Emma Monkey.

"But I know him," said Jake once more, almost in a whisper.

That evening, before bedtime, Jake held his monkey sticker in his hand and whispered a quiet prayer, "Spelladictionary Monkey, wherever you are, thank you. I know that you are real, you are real to me. I can spell now because of you. Thank you for sharing your secret place and special spelling tricks with me."

Jake had a beautiful dream that night. He dreamt that he was in a spelling competition at school and that he could spell every word perfectly.

The End

Acknowledgements

Mum and dad, for always looking after me.

Gail, Nanda and Carole for all the 'spelling chats'.

Emma, for creating such a wonderful Jake!

Paul and Lewis for producing the story, 'Jake Monkey-Tail'.

Jess, for helping me in every way.

To all my friends, little and big, who have been excited to meet Jake.